Movie Mystery

by Christine Peymani

Bath · New York · Singapore · Hong Kong · Cologne · Delhi · Melbourne

First published by Parragon in 2007
Parragon
Queen Street House
4 Queen Street
Bath BA1 1HE, UK

ISBN 978-1-4054-9961-3

Printed in the UK

CHAPTER 1

"Okay girls, we've got to get this magazine wrapped up," Jade announced.

She looked around the offices of Bratz Magazine, the publication she'd started with her best friends Cloe, Sasha and Yasmin.

Cloe was examining photos on her computer screen, making her final picks to illustrate their feature stories. Yasmin was typing rapidly, finishing an article of hers that they were publishing in this issue. Sasha was checking the final layout, making sure that everything fitted together and that their advertisers all had the placements they'd paid for. And Jade had just got off the phone with their printer, who was pushing for them to get the magazine over there right away.

"How much time do we have left?" Sasha asked, without pausing to look away from her computer.

"One hour," Jade replied. "Can we do it, girls?"

"Of course!" Cloe agreed. "Except ... I can't decide between these different shots for our winter fashion spread. I mean, the model looks better in this one, but I think this one shows off the dress better. But then, there's a cool background in this one – or we could use the group shot, here–"

"Let me see," Jade interrupted, peering over Cloe's shoulder at the photos displayed on the screen. "I like that one," she declared, pointing to a snapshot of a model in a deep purple dress, posing

2

with her hands on her hips. "It has an awesome sense of attitude."

"Done!" Cloe said, relieved. She dragged the photo over to the fashion-spread layout and smiled. "That looks gorgeous. Good call, Jade!"

"Just doing my job," Jade told her. Jade had always dreamed of working at a fashion magazine, and when the girls had decided to start their own, Jade had been the obvious choice to be its editor. "Anyone else need anything?"

"We have this Betsey Lederhosen ad that came in at the last minute," Sasha replied, showing Jade an image from one of their favourite fashion designer's new clothing line. "She's a huge advertiser for us, so I really want to find her a spot if we can. But the rest of the magazine looks so fabulous that I don't really want to move anything around."

"Okay, let's add a promo for our next issue," Jade began. "We have the cover ready, right?"

Sasha nodded, pulling up a cover featuring a hot new movie star. She dropped it into the template they used for their magazine promos, which read 'Check Out the Latest from Bratz Magazine!' Leaning over Sasha's shoulder, Jade nodded her approval of the new promo page. "But then we need to add two more pages, or the page count won't come out right."

"Cloe, do you have enough photos to add a second spread to the Winter Wonderland fashion piece?" Jade asked.

"Absolutely!" Cloe agreed. "That would be perfect, actually, because we have tons of cute shots here that I really don't want to cut out."

"Yasmin, can you whip up a few extra

captions for us if Cloe picks the photos right now?" Jade turned to Yasmin, who finished typing with a flourish and spun around in her wheeled office chair.

"No problem," Yasmin declared. "I just finished this article, so I can start on those captions right now. But Jade, would you read over this piece while I write up some captions?"

"I'd love to," Jade said. Yasmin printed out her article, while Jade helped Cloe pick out a few more photos for their fashion piece.

Cloe emailed the shots they picked to Yasmin, who started writing short descriptions of the outfits.

"Sasha, do you have the details on who designed these clothes, and where to buy them and everything?" Yasmin asked.

Sasha joined Yasmin at her computer and checked out the new images. "Sure - let me go and grab them."

Because the girls loved to shop as much as their readers did, they knew how important it was to include information on where to buy the hip new looks they showcased every month.

Sasha picked up the binder where she'd organized photos of each item of clothing they had photographed for this issue, with designer and 'where to buy' information listed on the back of each one. She returned to Yasmin's desk and flipped quickly through the pages of photos, pulling out the ones that Yasmin needed to write the extra captions.

Jade sat on the edge of her own desk, reading Yasmin's article.

"Yas, this is fantastic!" Jade announced after a moment.

"You really think so?" Yasmin asked.

"Absolutely," Jade assured her.

"Well, I hope you'll feel the same way about these captions," Yasmin said. "Cloe, I just emailed them to you so you can pair them with the photos."

"Got 'em," Cloe replied. She cut and pasted the captions into the layout, then printed out the new spread. Jade grabbed the printout and scanned it quickly, a smile spreading across her face.

"You guys, this spread is incredible!" Jade declared. "I can't believe you whipped it up in just a few minutes!"

"With your help," Cloe pointed out.

"What can I say?" Sasha added. "We make an amazing team."

Sasha added the fashion spread to the final layout, with the Betsey Lederhosen and Bratz Magazine ads right after it.

"Looks good to me," she announced. "Jade, do you want to look through it one last time?"

"If you say it's good, I'm sure it is," Jade told her. "But sure, it's always good to have a second pair of eyes on something."

She clicked through each spread of the magazine on Sasha's computer, pausing to examine the overall look of each page. Yasmin and Cloe hurried over and clustered around the screen so they could get one last look at the finished product, too.

When Jade reached the last page, she paused, and

her friends waited anxiously for her verdict. They were happy with all the pieces they'd put together, but just hoped that everything had come together perfectly.

"So, what do you think?" Sasha asked after a moment. "Can we send it to the printer?"

"I have to say it's the best issue of Bratz Magazine yet!" Jade declared.

"You say that every month," Yasmin teased.

"But it's always true!" Jade insisted.

"Okay, I'm sending it," Sasha announced. She burned the huge document that made up their whole magazine onto a disc while Jade called for a messenger.

"So now we celebrate, right?" Cloe asked.

Their office phone rang, and Jade grabbed it. "Bratz Magazine, this is Jade."

Her friends watched as her eyes widened and her jaw dropped. They crowded around her, eager to find out who was on the other end of the line.

CHAPTER 2

Jade hung up the phone and turned to face her friends, her green eyes gleaming with excitement.

"So, who was it?" Cloe asked eagerly.

"Ooh, was it one of the hip-hop artists we wanted to profile for the next issue?" Sasha interrupted.

"Or one of the designers we were planning to feature?" Yasmin added.

"Or an invitation to a spectacular party we need to cover?" Cloe suggested.

"Even better," Jade replied. "That was Isabella Rivera, who runs the Starshine Film Festival."

"You mean the hottest festival of the year?" Sasha cried.

"Where all the coolest, most cutting-edge movies premiere?" Yasmin interjected.

"And all the hippest stars show up to hit the spectacular party scene?" Cloe squealed.

"Exactly," Jade told them. "And of course it's held at the most luxurious ski resort in the country."

"So why was she calling us?" Yasmin asked.

"She said she wants to give the four of us all-access passes for the entire festival, plus invites to all the best after-parties, so we can cover the whole thing for Bratz Magazine," Jade explained.

"Omigosh!" her friends exclaimed in unison, jumping up and down.

"So, do you want to go?" Jade asked, raising her eyebrows. "Or should I tell her we can't make it?"

"Call her back right now and tell her we're in!" Cloe demanded.

"It's okay, Cloe. I already said yes," Jade admitted. "It was too exciting an opportunity to turn down."

"It sure is!" Yasmin agreed. "I've always dreamed of going to Starshine. We'll get to meet lots of amazing directors and writers, and see the most wonderful new movies before anyone else. I can't believe we're actually going!"

"So when do we leave?" Sasha asked.

"Well, that's the thing," Jade replied. "Luckily, the festival mostly falls during our winter break. But we need to leave on Friday so we can be there in time for the Saturday premieres."

"But that's the last day of class before break," Yasmin protested. "We have finals that day."

"So, we'll just have to take them early," Cloe declared. "I mean, we can't let our readers down!"

"We'll have to see what our teachers say," Sasha pointed out. "The magazine's important, but school has to come first."

"Of course," Jade agreed. "We'll talk to them first thing in the morning. I'm sure we can work something out."

The messenger dashed through the front door of their office suite and Sasha handed over the disc. When he left, Cloe cried, "So now can we go and celebrate wrapping our latest issue?"

"Yes, Cloe," Jade said with a laugh.

The girls hurried out to treat themselves to dinner for a job well done – and to talk about their upcoming adventure at the Starshine Film Festival!

The girls couldn't wait to get to school that Monday morning so they could share their exciting news with all their friends, and get their teachers' permission to start their break a day early.

They found their maths teacher, Mr Gonzales and their biology teacher, Miss Couri, sitting in front of the school eating bagels.

"Sorry to interrupt, but we have a really important question," Sasha gasped, rushing up to the two teachers.

"What can we do for you, Sasha?" Mr Gonzales asked, smiling.

"Well, we've been invited to the Starshine Film Festival, but we

©MGA

have to leave on Friday," Jade explained. "So we were wondering if maybe we could take our finals in both of your classes on Thursday instead?"

"We'll stay after school, or come in over lunch, or whatever you want," Yasmin added.

"Please, there has to be some way we can make this work," Cloe interrupted.

"Wow, I don't think I've ever heard anyone be so eager to take a test early," Miss Couri said with a grin. "But sure, if you're up for it, it's fine with me."

"Same here," Mr Gonzales agreed.

"Thank you so much!" Cloe cried.

"I hope our other teachers are as cool about this as you two," Jade said.

As it turned out, most of them were. The girls would have to come in early and stay after school every day for the rest of the week, but at least they'd be able to make it to the festival in time. But when they tracked down the last teacher, Mrs Ackerman, in their world history classroom, she was not so thrilled with the idea.

"Girls, I'm sorry, but I have obligations before and after school every day this week, and lunchtime simply won't give you enough time to complete the whole test," Mrs Ackerman explained.

"But there must be something we can do!" Cloe wailed. "I mean, we have to be at the festival on Saturday!"

"What if we sat in on your first class on Friday and took our final then?" Yasmin suggested. "Then we can head to the airport right after the test."

"Well, I guess that could work," Mrs Ackerman replied. "I mean, I'd hate to be the reason you couldn't get to the festival in time

... so, yes, why don't you join my first class on Friday? Great idea, Yasmin."

"We can't thank you enough," Jade gushed.

"We'll bring you a Starshine souvenir as a thank you if you want," Cloe added.

"Oh, you don't have to do that," Mrs Ackerman protested. "Just bring back lots of stories about the festival and all the cool celebrities you see there!"

"We can definitely do that," Yasmin agreed.

The bell rang, announcing that it was almost time for school to start, and the girls waved goodbye to their teacher and headed for their first classes.

"We did it, girls!" Sasha declared in the hallway. "We're going to Starshine!"

CHAPTER 3

"You know we're going to need some truly glamorous clothes to really stand out at the festival," Jade said that afternoon on the drive home from school. "Anyone up for a shopping trip?"

"No!" her friends exclaimed, and Jade looked at them in surprise.

"Jade, we have so much studying to do," Sasha explained. "We have, like, six finals in the next three days."

"Plus I have to finish my big art project," Cloe added.

"I have a story to write for my creative-writing final," Yasmin chimed in.

"And I need to prepare a solo for my final in choir," Sasha said.

"Yeah, I have to turn in a magazine design for my journalism class," Jade admitted. "Though that shouldn't be hard, with Bratz Magazine experience."

"True," Yasmin agreed. "But we need all the time we can get to finish everything in time."

"Well, I guess we have enough outfits in our wardrobes already," Jade replied. "I'm sure we can put something fabulous together."

"I'm sure," Cloe said. "If we aren't too exhausted by all that test-taking to come up with cute new looks."

"We've always managed before," Sasha declared. "I'm sure we can do it this time."

"That's the spirit!" Yasmin cried. "But for now, let's get to work!"

The girls barely had time to talk all week long, between all the studying and test-taking. Whenever she had a spare moment, Jade was on the phone to Isabella at Starshine, planning out the details of their trip, from where to stay to which films to see and which parties to go to. And with each conversation, she got increasingly excited about their trip.

On Wednesday afternoon, after taking their maths final, the girls met up at Jade's place to finish studying for their history final, go over their schedule and plan their outfits for the week ahead.

When Jade told them everything they'd be doing, Cloe flopped dramatically onto her friend's bed, miming exhaustion.

"And I thought this was supposed to be a holiday!" she sighed.

"At least we'll have the second week of break to recover," Yasmin pointed out.

"But we'll be busy with our families for the holidays that week," Sasha reminded them. "It won't exactly be relaxing."

"It'll all be fun, though," Jade said, and her friends nodded in agreement. She gestured to the suitcases the girls had lined up just inside her door. "Okay, ladies, let's see what you've got."

"Are you sure we shouldn't get in a little more studying first?" Yasmin asked anxiously. "I mean, Mrs Ackerman's tests are really hard."

"I don't think my brain can absorb one more historical fact right now," Cloe protested. "Let's at least take a study break."

"I guess we could do that," Yasmin agreed.

"Great!" Cloe cried. "Because I have some spectacular stuff to show you girls!" She flung open her suitcase and pulled out a short, silky, cherry-red dress. "I thought this would be perfect for the big premiere party on Saturday night."

"That's utterly stunning," Jade declared.

"And I know it's cold there, so I packed some jeans and cosy sweaters, too," Cloe continued. She held up a black wrap sweater trimmed with cheetah-print faux fur and her friends sighed.

"You'll be super-stylin' and super-warm," Sasha cried. "The perfect Starshine combination!"

"So you think I'm on the right track?" Cloe asked. "Because I'm still trying to figure out the rest of my outfits for the festival."

"Keep going like you're going, and you'll totally steal the spotlight at this festival!" Jade told her.

"Thanks, Jade," Cloe said, relieved. "Now

let's see what you came up with."

"Okay, first my favourite glam look," Jade began, grabbing a long-sleeved sheath dress from her wardrobe that perfectly matched her bright green eyes.

"Love it!" Sasha squealed.

"So what did you choose for a warmer look?" Yasmin asked.

"I thought I'd pair thigh-high boots with skinny jeans," Jade told them. "I love this button-down shirt and vest combo, so I'll definitely wear this for one of the days."

"You always have the best fashion ideas," Cloe gushed. "I wish you could just plan my whole wardrobe for me!"

"You don't do so bad yourself," Jade pointed out. "All right, who's up next?"

"I have this new sweater that I'm crazy about," Sasha interjected. She showed her friends a periwinkle sweater with ruffles at the collar and sleeves. "I'll just wear this with jeans, too."

"You'll look super-sweet in that!" Yasmin cried. "And after the festival, can I borrow it?"

"Definitely," Sasha agreed. "And here's one of my fancier looks." She laid out a sky-blue turtleneck sweater dress with puffed sleeves on the bed and added, "I'm planning to give it some edge with tall boots like Jade's."

"How cool," Jade told her. "Okay, Yas, you're up."

©MGA

"Well, first, I found this shirt," she said, holding up a leaf-green fitted shirt with billowing sleeves. "And I thought it would look chic with black trousers and knee-high tan-coloured boots."

"That sounds fabulous," Sasha announced.

"Thanks, Sash," Yasmin replied modestly. "And then, well ... I fell in love with this little purple dress."

She shyly pulled the dress out of her bag and the girls all gasped.

"Wow, Yas, you out-glammed all of us," Jade declared. "I love this off-the-shoulder style."

She grabbed the dress and admired its silhouette – short skirt, ruched down the side, with a single shoulder strap tied in a bow.

"You don't think it's too much?" Yasmin

asked, peering up at her friends through her thick eyelashes.

"At Starshine, I don't think there's such a thing as too much!" Cloe exclaimed. "It's the perfect chance to strut your stuff!"

"That's good," Yasmin said, "because I can't wait to wear that dress!"

"Now that we're all on the same fashion page, should we get in a little more studying?" Sasha asked.

The girls all groaned, but grabbed their textbooks and got back to studying for their last final.

CHAPTER 4

Cloe picked up her friends for school in the morning, and they all loaded their suitcases into the boot of her cruiser so they could head straight for the airport after they finished their final.

"I'm so tired," Cloe complained.

"Me too," Yasmin agreed. "But we just have to get through this one last test, and then we're off to Starshine!"

"I'm sure all the movies, parties and skiing will totally revive us," Jade added. "I mean, we'll be having too much fun to be tired!"

But the girls definitely felt tired during world history that morning. They'd been working so hard all week that they were all totally burned out. After they handed in their tests and burst into the hallway, the four best friends exchanged worried looks.

"She wasn't kidding about that test being hard," Yasmin said.

"I'm sure we did fine," Sasha insisted. "We studied hard, and I'm sure we knew our stuff."

"Well, you probably did," Cloe grumbled. "You're great at history."

"I guess we'll just have to see when we get back," Jade interrupted. "But for now, let's focus on this fabulous film festival we're headed for."

"Woo-hoo!" the girls cheered as they piled into Cloe's car.

"Starshine, here we come!" Cloe added, finally perking up as she slid behind the wheel.

"It's so beautiful here!" Yasmin murmured when they landed in Snow Summit, Colorado, where the festival was held every year. She peered out of the window of the plane at the snow-covered mountains, sparkling so brightly in the sunlight that they appeared to have been sprinkled with glitter.

"Ooh, I can't wait to hit those slopes!" Cloe added.

"We have to meet with Isabella to get all the press materials and tickets and everything first," Jade reminded her. "And we have that Cougar Studios party tonight. But maybe we'll have time for a little skiing in-between."

She and her friends picked up their hand luggage and filed off the plane, eager to get their trip started.

"We're here all week," Sasha interjected. "I'm sure we can fit in some time on the slopes before we go."

"Don't you think we should include an article on skiing in our Starshine Special Issue?" Cloe insisted. "I mean, it is held at the top ski resort in the world."

"If we're doing that, we should definitely cover snowboarding too," Yasmin suggested. "It's a totally hip sport that I know a lot of our readers are into."

"Good thinking, Yas!" Jade agreed as they strode through the terminal towards the luggage carousel. "We should definitely do a winter sports feature."

The girls spotted their bags on the carousel and grabbed them, then headed outside, where Isabella had said they could catch a Starshine Shuttle.

But Sasha stopped in her tracks besides the automatic doors, feeling the cold seep through the glass.

"What's wrong, Sash?" Yasmin asked. "Did you forget something?"

"Sasha never forgets anything," Jade pointed out.

"That may be true. I almost forgot that it's way colder here than back home, and that we had all better wrap up warm before we go out there so we don't freeze!" Sasha explained.

The girls zipped up their puffy winter coats, wrapped fuzzy scarves around their necks and pulled on their insulated gloves.

"Now I'm definitely ready to hit the slopes!" Cloe declared.

But even with all those layers, the girls were still stunned by the gust of cold wind that hit them when they stepped outside.

"It's gorgeous here," Yasmin said, "but it's way too cold."

The shuttle dropped them off at the Starshine Ski Resort, the huge lodge nestling at the foot of the mountains where the four girls were staying.

"Check it out – you can literally step out of the front door and hop right on the ski lift!" Jade pointed out, gesturing towards other guests who were doing just that.

"Not a bad location," Yasmin agreed.

The girls trooped over to the front desk and Jade announced to the receptionist, "We're with Bratz Magazine – you should have a room for us."

"Ah, yes," the woman said, smiling. "We were able to put you in a mountain-view room. I hope you'll enjoy your stay!"

She handed over four copies of the room's key-card and the girls headed for the lift, talking excitedly.

"We're really getting the royal treatment here!" Cloe exclaimed.

"Well, Isabella said that most of the movies premiering here this year are perfectly targeted to our magazine's audience, so she wanted to make sure that we were here to cover this," Jade explained.

"It's a tough job, but someone has to do it," Sasha declared as they threw open the door to their hotel room.

The room was huge, with two king-size beds covered

©MGA

in fluffy quilts and a gorgeous view of the mountains through its big picture window.

"Wow, those beds look really good right now," Cloe said, hopping onto the one closest to her. "I'm beat!"

"No time for napping," Jade protested. "We have to get to our meeting with Isabella!"

"I know, I know," Cloe grumbled.

She and her friends unpacked quickly, making themselves at home in the room, then headed back out to meet the woman who had brought them there.

"Welcome to Starshine, ladies!" Isabella Rivera cried, hurrying out from behind her large oak desk and hugging each of them in turn. With her dark bob and elegant black trouser suit, she looked utterly chic. "I am a huge fan of your magazine, and I couldn't be happier to have you here covering our festival!"

"We're thrilled to be here, too," Jade began, but Isabella was talking so rapidly that she didn't seem to notice that Jade had spoken.

"First, here are your all-access passes for the movies," Isabella continued, grabbing from her desk four cords with Starshine passes dangling from the ends and draping them around each girl's neck. "You can see anything you want – and there's tons of great stuff to see here!"

"I'm sure, Ms Rivera," Yasmin interjected. "We're eager to review all the cutting-edge films that–"

"Please, call me Isabella!" their host exclaimed. "And you won't just be seeing movies – these wristbands will get you into any party you want to attend." She fastened a purple wristband around each girl's wrist and added, "And believe me, there are plenty of awesome parties to check out!"

"Thank you so much," Sasha said. "We're really looking forward to-"

"Now don't forget to come by the Cougar Studios party tonight," Isabella interrupted. "It's the official start of the festival, and everyone who's anyone will be there - including you, of course!" She looked at her watch and added, "Well, it's been lovely to meet you, but now I'd better run - this is my busiest week of the year! Ta-ta!"

And with that, she dashed out of her office, leaving the four best friends to stare after her in amazement.

"And you guys say I talk a lot," Cloe murmured.

"She's just enthusiastic about what she does," Yasmin replied. "You have to admire that."

"I totally do," Sasha said.

"So, should we go and get ready for the party, so everyone can admire us?" Jade suggested.

"Oh yeah!" her best friends agreed happily.

CHAPTER 5

"This is utterly glam!" Cloe declared when they stepped into the huge ballroom at the lodge, where the evening's party was being held.

The walls were draped in lush burgundy fabric and the room sparkled with candles that flickered on every table. The party's theme was 'A Night at the Movies', and there were screens everywhere showing clips from famous movies, while waiters and waitresses in cinema usher costumes offered guests tiny portions of popcorn and sweets.

At the far end of the room, brightly coloured lights flashed above the dance floor, which was already crowded with people jamming to the pop grooves that blasted from the speakers.

"Do you girls want to dance?" Sasha asked.

"Always!" her friends exclaimed.

But as they made their way towards the dance floor, Yasmin spotted someone she recognized and pulled her friends to the side, whispering, "Look, it's Mia Mackenzie!"

"Who's that?" Cloe asked.

"Only the hottest young star in Hollywood!" Jade explained.

"She starred in my favourite movie last year, 'Summertime'," Yasmin added. "And she's here to promote her very first indie movie."

"Let's go and get an interview," Sasha suggested.

©MGA

They headed for the table where Mia was standing, but when they were almost there, Yasmin stopped suddenly.

"We can't just walk up to her," she protested. "I mean, she's like, a huge star."

"So what?" Cloe replied. "We're the editors of Bratz Magazine – we meet stars all the time."

"But I totally admire her," Yasmin continued. "Why don't you girls go on? I'll wait here."

"Yas, she's just a person, and actually, she looks really lonely right now," Jade said.

Yasmin glanced over and noticed that the actress was standing all alone, looking around anxiously as though she was waiting for someone.

"She'd probably be happy to have some company," Sasha added.

"You're probably right," Yasmin admitted.

The girls walked up to Mia and introduced themselves.

"You run Bratz Magazine?" she asked, and when they nodded, she cried, "I love Bratz Magazine!"

While the girls smiled modestly, Mia continued, "I love your dresses." The girls were all decked out in the glitzy gowns they'd shown off to each other the night before. "You all look so glamorous!"

"We feel glamorous just being here at Starshine," Cloe gushed.

"Is this your first Starshine Festival?" she asked, and when the girls nodded, she squealed, "Mine too!"

"I hear the movie you're in is great," Yasmin said shyly.

"I hope the judges agree!" Mia cried.

"Winning a Starshine award would be huge for me."

"You totally deserve one," Yasmin told her, and Mia smiled.

"Well, you have to come to the premiere tomorrow night so you can see for yourself," she said.

"We're there!" Jade agreed.

Just then, one of the girls' favourite songs blared out of the speakers that lined the dance floor, and they all squealed with excitement.

"Let's dance!" Sasha exclaimed.

"Do you want to join us?" Jade asked Mia, and she nodded eagerly, following them onto the dance floor. Soon she was learning all of Sasha's coolest dance moves, and the five girls spent all evening talking and laughing together. Mia introduced them to lots of other celebrities, and although Jade snapped a ton of pictures for their magazine, they were having way too much fun with her to be star-struck by all the famous faces.

"I'm so glad I met you girls," Mia said, giving each of her new friends a hug at the end of the night. "You really made this party a blast!"

"I can't believe we just hung out with Mia Mackenzie," Yasmin whispered to her friends as they headed back to their hotel room.

"That's Starshine magic at work!" Cloe declared.

The next day, the girls hit one movie premiere after another, but they couldn't wait to see their new friend Mia that night at the premiere of her movie, *On the Edge*.

"I can't believe we get to watch movies all day long," Jade told her friends.

"I know – this is, like, the coolest place ever!" Cloe added.

They were already starting to get used to the cold, and were actually enjoying the chance to wrap up in their cute ski jackets.

"So does everyone have notes on all the movies we've seen so far?" Sasha asked as they headed for their last movie of the day.

"Of course," Yasmin replied. "This is tons of fun, but we are here on assignment."

"Our next issue of Bratz Magazine will be the guide to all the hottest new movies on the scene," Jade declared.

"You know it," Cloe agreed.

"Well, I was just thinking we should start compiling some of our reviews, and–" Sasha began, but Jade interrupted her.

"Remember, we're here to have fun, too," Jade said. "We can always type up our notes

45

back in Stilesville, but how often do we get to hang out at a fabulous film festival?"

"She has a point, Sasha," Yasmin chimed in. "Anyway, we need more material before we can decide what we should include. Especially since we haven't even seen the coolest movie at the festival yet!"

With that, she burst through the doors of an old-fashioned cinema, with gilt-edged mouldings decorating the ceiling and lush red carpeting on the floors. "But we're about to!" she added, as she and her best friends made their way through the throng of people waiting to see Mia's new film.

Cloe spotted Mia from across the room and ran over to her, giving her a big hug. "We can't wait to see your movie!" she squealed.

"I hope you'll like it," Mia said worriedly.

"I'm sure we will," Yasmin insisted.

Just then, a tall young man with dark,

wavy hair appeared beside Mia.

"Ladies, I'd like you to meet Xavier Redman, the amazing director of *On the Edge*!" said Mia.

Xavier shook each of the girl's hands and announced, "Any friend of Mia's is a friend of mine! But I'll have to tear Mia away from you in a minute so we can introduce the movie together."

"I guess we can allow that," Jade said, smiling at the cute director.

"See you in there," he replied with a wave as he strolled across the lobby.

©MGA

47

When he paused to talk to a group of actors, Sasha asked Mia, "Hey, who's that guy following Xavier?"

"Where?" Mia followed Sasha's gaze to a skinny blond guy who was skulking behind a column and peering out at Xavier. "Oh, him? That's Cole Larkin. He's a director too. In fact, his first film is premiering here tomorrow."

"So why's he spying on Xavier?" Yasmin asked.

"Who knows?" Mia shrugged and headed into the cinema with the girls following her. "He's been following Xavier ever since we got here. I mean, Xavier is the hottest young director around – maybe Cole's hoping some of that coolness will rub off on him."

Mia strode to the front of the cinema, while her friends grabbed seats towards the centre. The lights dimmed, and everyone scrambled for a seat. Xavier and Mia took the stage, and the audience cheered.

"I'm happy to present the world premiere of my new film, *On the Edge*," Xavier announced. "Enjoy, and stick around afterwards for a question-and-answer session with me, plus the star of my movie, Mia Mackenzie!"

Xavier and Mia sat down while the audience applauded, and the movie screen flickered to life.

"This is gonna be so great!" Cloe whispered, and her friends all nodded, their eyes fixed on the screen. But when they saw what appeared there, they turned to each other, stunned.

"Is that part of Xavier's movie?" Jade asked her friends. "Because it looks more like a home movie."

Onscreen were shots of two little girls splashing in a paddling pool, jumping into piles of brightly coloured leaves and pushing each other on the swings at a playground. The shots were very cute, but it wasn't exactly high art.

Xavier leapt back onto the stage and shouted, "Stop the projector! That isn't my movie!"

A surprised murmur spread through the crowd as the screen went black.

CHAPTER 6

Isabella stepped onstage and held her hands up to quieten the crowd.

"We're experiencing some technical difficulties," she began, "so we're going to have to reschedule this screening."

Everyone in the audience groaned in response, but began gathering their coats and making their way out of the cinema.

Cloe, Jade, Sasha and Yasmin rushed to the stage, where Mia looked ready to burst into tears. Xavier was pacing back and forth, tugging at his wavy hair and muttering, "What am I going to do?" Isabella was on her mobile phone, barking commands as she tried to work out what had gone wrong.

The projectionist, a black-haired man in

glasses, bolted down the aisle to join them.

"I don't know what happened!" he cried. "The reel was marked *On the Edge*, and it looked exactly like the reel I did a test run with this afternoon. But that definitely wasn't the movie I saw this afternoon!"

"No, it wasn't!" Xavier shouted. "That was someone's cheesy home movie, not the important film I made!"

"Now, now," Isabella said soothingly. "We're all very upset, but I'm sure our projectionist had nothing to do with it. Derrick here has been with us since this festival first began, and we've never had a problem like this before."

"Isn't there another copy somewhere?" Sasha asked.

"Back at my office in Los Angeles," Xavier replied. "We'll have to have it shipped."

"Which means that unless we find those

reels, we'll have to wait a couple more days to premiere this movie," Isabella added. "And the festival schedule is pretty packed, so I just don't know how we'll fit it in."

Xavier moaned, hiding his head in his hands.

"How can this be happening?" he cried.

"Don't worry, Xavier," Cloe declared, "we'll find that missing movie!"

He turned to her in surprise. "Um, aren't you fashion magazine reporters?"

"Well, yeah," Cloe admitted. "But we've solved a mystery or two in our day. And I'm sure we can solve this one."

"Omigosh, you're my heroes!" Mia cried. Her face was streaked with tears as she hugged each of her new friends in turn.

"Ooh, I knew it was a good idea to bring you girls to the festival!" Isabella exclaimed.

"See, Xavier? Everything's going to be just fine, now that these bright young ladies are on the case!"

"We'll see about that," Xavier grumbled under his breath. No one heard him except Sasha, who motioned her friends to the side.

"I know he's upset," she whispered, "but don't you think Xavier's over-reacting a little?"

"Maybe," Yasmin replied. "But, I mean, this could have ruined his chances at the festival. I'd be pretty upset too."

"True," Sasha agreed. "But I think we should keep an eye on him. Something doesn't seem quite right."

The girls nodded, then rejoined the rest of the group.

"Okay, first we need to search the projection booth," Sasha announced, taking control of the situation as she often did.

"I already looked everywhere," Derrick protested, but Isabella shook her head at him warningly and he added, "but it's always good to get a second opinion. Or third, fourth, or fifth."

"Then let's go!" Jade said, and Derrick led the way back up the aisle.

Behind them, a flock of reporters surged around Mia, Xavier and Isabella to get the scoop on the missing movie. Peering over her shoulder at them, Yasmin noticed that the actress, director and festival organizer all seemed to perk right up once they were surrounded by cameras and microphones.

"You don't really think any of them would have sabotaged their own screening, do you?" Yasmin whispered to her friends while Derrick walked ahead, leading the way up to the projection booth through the stragglers who were still wandering out of the cinema.

"I don't know," Sasha told her, "but we're going to find out."

When they reached the projection booth, the girls were amazed to see so many film reels crammed into such a tiny space.

"This is where the magic happens," Derrick declared.

"Everything looks so small from up here," Jade said, gazing down at the cinema below through the window at the front of the booth.

"So can we see the reel that played tonight?" Sasha asked.

"Sure," Derrick agreed. "It's still in the projector."

He unthreaded the film and handed Sasha the reel.

©MGA

"It looks professional," Yasmin said, inspecting it. "Not like a typical home movie."

"This never would've happened if it looked like a home movie," Derrick insisted. "Someone went to a lot of trouble to get a fake reel in here."

"Could anyone else have got in here today?" Jade asked.

"Nope. Besides the master key Isabella keeps in her office, I have the only key to this booth, and it's always right here," he explained, patting the front pocket of his jeans.

"Well, did anyone come up while you were here?" Cloe prodded.

"Just Cole Larkin," Derrick said with a shrug.

"The director?" Yasmin asked. The girls exchanged glances, certain they'd found their first suspect.

"He loves being in the projection booth, just like I do," Derrick replied. "Best seat in the house, in my opinion."

"Did he bring anything with him?" Sasha wanted to know.

"Well, he always carries a black messenger bag - he keeps his latest scripts and stuff in there," Derrick told them.

"Is it big enough to hold a film reel?" Yasmin insisted.

Derrick stared out of the window, looking thoughtful. "Well, sure, I guess so. But you don't think Cole is behind this, do you? No, no way - he's crazy about this festival. He'd never do anything to mess it up."

"Not even if it could knock his biggest competitor for the best director prize out of the race?" Cloe demanded.

Derrick shook his head. "Not Cole. I just

can't see him doing something like that."

"I can," Cloe whispered, so softly that only her friends heard.

They thanked Derrick for his time and headed back to the cinema's main floor, determined to find Cole and get some answers.

CHAPTER 7

By the time they got downstairs, the cinema was deserted, and they had no clue how to find Cole.

"Maybe we should get some rest and start fresh tomorrow," Sasha suggested, and her friends agreed.

When they reached their hotel room, there was a phone message waiting for them from Mia.

"I was wondering if you girls might be free to go skiing tomorrow," she said. "Hitting the slopes always cheers me up when I'm down." They heard some sniffles on the recording as she added, "And I'm totally down right now."

She sounded so sad that Yasmin called her

back right away and promised that they would all meet her in the lobby first thing in the morning. The girls quickly changed into their flannel pyjamas, washed their faces and then flopped onto their cushy beds and fell asleep right away, exhausted from their long day of movie-going.

The next morning, the girls woke up early and pulled on their ski trousers, ski jackets, knitted hats and fleece-lined gloves. They trooped down to the lobby and found Mia looking sporty chic in her pink-and-cream ski gear.

"Even all wrapped up from head to toe, you girls manage to look totally cute!" Mia exclaimed.

"Same to you," Jade replied.

At the front of the lobby, the ski lodge offered rentals of all the equipment they would need – skis, boots and poles. Each girl bought a half-day pass and then they headed outside, where they strapped on their skis so they could hop on the lift that went right past the resort.

"You girls pair up," Mia told them. "I'll grab the last chair on my own."

"Are you sure?" Yasmin asked. "I mean, we're here to cheer you up – I don't want to leave you alone."

"I think I can manage a little ride to the top," Mia insisted. "And then we'll all ski down together!"

The girls all jumped onto the lift and peered down at the gorgeous, snow-covered mountainside that flashed below them, their breath appearing in white puffs in the cold air.

"Look at how high up we are!" Cloe squealed.

"It's incredible," Jade agreed.

Then they were at the top, and they skied down the mountain, the chilly wind whipping through their hair as they zoomed down the slope.

"That was awesome!" Mia declared when they reached the bottom. "I feel better already!"

"We really are going to find that movie," Sasha assured her. "After we've finished skiing, we're planning to track down Cole Larkin. We think he just might know something about what happened yesterday."

"Do you really think Cole could've done something like that?" Mia asked, her hazel eyes wide.

"We won't know until we ask him," Yasmin explained, "but yeah, he seems like a pretty good suspect."

"Maybe you should go and find him right now," Mia suggested. "I don't want to keep you from your investigation."

"Nah, let's get in a few more runs first," Jade replied. "We've got plenty of time to corner Cole."

"If you insist!" Mia hopped back on the lift and the others followed, giggling as they were swept up into the air.

"Let's try a different run this time," Sasha suggested. The girls skied over to a more difficult slope and started down.

But suddenly, a gangly man with a black ski mask covering his face zipped towards them.

"Watch out!" Cloe shouted, but it was too late. The man skied right into Mia, knocking her over, then sped away down the slope. Cloe, Jade and Yasmin skidded to a stop beside Mia, sending a spray of snow into the air.

"Hey!" Sasha yelled after the man in the ski mask. "Get back here!" She skied after him while her friends helped Mia up, but by the time she reached the bottom, he was out of sight.

Back on the slope, Cloe, Jade and Yasmin clustered around Mia, trying to make sure she was okay.

"Really, I'm fine," she insisted. "A little freaked out, but fine."

"I don't know," Yasmin said. "We'd better get you to a doctor."

"Do you think you can make it down the rest of the slope?" Cloe asked worriedly. "Or maybe I should call the ski patrol. They could send a helicopter or something to get you down, and-"

"That's okay – I think I can make it without a helicopter," Mia said, laughing.

"Well, if you're sure," Cloe replied reluctantly. The four girls continued down the slope and found Sasha waiting for them at the bottom.

"Did you find him?" Jade asked.

"No." Sasha shook her head dejectedly. "He was too fast for me."

"It's okay, Sasha," Yasmin said, putting her arm around her friend. "You did the best you could."

"But now how will we ever figure out who he

©MGA

was?" Sasha moaned.

"Oh, I think I have a pretty good idea," Jade announced. "He was tall and skinny - exactly like another suspicious guy we know."

"Cole!" Cloe gasped. "He's really out to get your movie, Mia!"

"Maybe you're right," Mia admitted as they reached the lodge.

A group of reporters hanging around the front desk noticed Mia limping in and rushed over to find out what was wrong. She started explaining about her mysterious attacker, and they whipped out their notebooks and pens, writing rapidly.

She was completely surrounded by reporters, and Sasha had to push her way through them to ask Mia, "Are you going to be okay? Because I think we'd better find Cole right away."

"No problem," Mia agreed. "Go get him,

girls!"

She turned back to the reporters and continued telling the story of how scared she'd been, and how she didn't know why anyone would want to hurt her, and she just hoped her injury wouldn't slow her down for the rest of the festival.

The girls hurried over to Isabella's office. Since she kept the official schedule for the whole festival, they were hoping she'd have some idea where they could find Cole.

"Of course I know where he is," Isabella told them. "His movie just premiered. He's doing a Q & A right now."

"That's impossible," Jade replied. "We just saw him on the ski slopes!"

Isabella checked her watch. "He's been answering questions for the past 15 minutes. If you want to talk to him, why don't you go over to the Royal Theatre so you can catch the tail end of his Q & A? You'd better hurry, though!"

"Thanks, Isabella!" the girls called as they hurried out of her office and down Main Street to the fancy cinema where Cole's movie had premiered.

"I bet he skipped the premiere," Cloe said, but when they burst into the cinema, the girls saw Cole sitting onstage, fielding questions from the crowd.

"I just wanted to make a movie that was really meaningful," he explained in a soft voice with a slight Southern accent. "I hope it felt that way to y'all."

The cinema manager rushed onstage and announced, "One last question!"

A hand shot up in the crowded cinema, and Cole pointed to a dark-haired woman. "Who would you most like to meet while you're here at Starshine?" she asked.

"Honestly, I'm hoping to meet the director Xavier Redman," Cole replied. "He's premiering his new movie here, and I can't wait to see it. I'm a big fan of his."

"I'm sure once he sees this movie, he'll be a fan of yours too," the cinema manager declared, and the audience burst into applause.

Cole stood and gave a funny little bow.

"I want to thank Cole for being here," the man continued, but Cole interrupted.

"I want to thank all of y'all for coming out to see my little film," he said. "It means a lot to have everyone here to watch something I made."

The audience clapped wildly as he headed offstage, waving as he left.

"He seems kind of sweet," Yasmin murmured to her friends.

"And he definitely wasn't on the slopes just now," Jade added.

"I'm not convinced," Sasha insisted.

"Then let's go and talk to him and get the scoop," Cloe suggested, and the girls hurried backstage, flashing their Bratz Magazine press passes to get past the guards.

CHAPTER 8

"Mr Larkin!" Cloe shouted. "Can we talk to you for a minute?"

He turned, pushing his glasses up his nose. "Of course. What can I do for you ladies?"

"We're from Bratz Magazine," Jade began, but Sasha stopped her with a shake of her head. She didn't want Cole to be on his guard when he talked to them.

"Is there somewhere we can sit down?" Sasha asked.

"Sure. Actually, my voice is a little shot from all that talking," Cole replied, "but I bet some hot chocolate would help. Would y'all care to join me?"

"I'm always up for hot chocolate!" Cloe

exclaimed. They followed Cole out of the cinema to a quaint little coffee shop next door.

"You girls grab a table, and I'll get hot chocolate for everyone," he said.

"Such a gentleman," Cloe whispered.

"I don't know," Sasha replied. "He seems a little too nice."

Cole returned with four steaming mugs of hot chocolate, topped with whipped cream and cinnamon, then went back to grab his own mug before joining the girls at their table.

"So, how can I help you?" he asked, leaning towards them.

"You were at the *On the Edge* premiere last

night, weren't you?" Jade began.

"Sure was," Cole agreed. "I wouldn't have missed it."

"Right, we heard you say you were a big Xavier fan," Yasmin interjected.

"Oh, I am," he replied. "I feel so bad for him about what happened."

"Do you have any idea how that could have happened?" Sasha demanded.

"I wish I did," Cole said, shaking his head sadly. "I was up in the projection booth right before it happened, but I had no idea anything was wrong."

The girls exchanged uncertain looks, and Cloe jumped in. "Have you been skiing lately?" she blurted out.

"Honestly?" Cole blushed, not meeting the girls' eyes. "I'm embarrassed to say that I actually don't know how to ski."

"You don't?" Cloe gasped.

"I know, it's ridiculous to be at such a great ski resort and not to know how to ski," he said, shaking his head sadly, "but I just never learned."

"Hey, don't feel bad," Yasmin protested. "I mean, skiing's really hard."

"Yeah, and directing a whole movie is way harder, and you can do that," Jade pointed out. "So don't get too down on yourself."

"Aw, thanks, girls," Cole said, giving them a shy smile.

"Okay, but we still have one more question for you," Sasha interrupted. Cole turned to her, and she blurted out, "Why have you been following Xavier around?"

He blushed even brighter red this time as he stammered, "Well – I – it's just ..." He sighed, and then admitted, "He's my favourite director, and I thought now that I have a film at Starshine too that I'd finally have the courage to go and meet him. But, well ... I didn't."

"So you've just been hanging around him because you were trying to work up the nerve to introduce yourself?" Cloe asked.

"Yeah ... pretty pathetic, huh?" he sighed.

"Not at all!" Yasmin told him. "Like, I totally admire Mia Mackenzie, but I was too scared to introduce myself to her. I never could've done it without my friends there to cheer me on."

"And we can cheer you on when you meet Xavier, too!" Cloe offered. "In fact, we can introduce you."

"Really?" Cole looked at the girls hopefully. "That would be so great."

"Absolutely," Sasha agreed. They had

finished their hot chocolate and began gathering up their things.

"But wait," Cole said. "Was that all you wanted to ask me?"

"Oh ..." Sasha looked away, embarrassed, but none of her friends spoke up, so she continued, "... well, we're trying to find out who's sabotaging Xavier's movie. See, first there was the missing reel, and then someone pushed Mia over on the slopes and, well ..."

"You thought it was me?" Cole asked.

"We're really sorry!" Cloe cried. "We didn't know how nice you were when we thought you were a suspect!"

"See, we knew you'd been up in the projection booth, and the guy who pushed Mia looked an awful lot like you," Jade explained. "And we thought you were hanging around Xavier because you were spying on him, or something."

"I can see how it looked suspicious," Cole replied. "I mean, I probably would've suspected me too. I'm just glad you ladies gave me the opportunity to clear my name."

"Let's go and find Xavier right now so we can introduce you two," Yasmin suggested. "And then you'll forgive us for suspecting you, right?"

"Of course," Cole said. "In fact, I'll be completely in your debt if you can help me finally meet Xavier."

"Well, come on then!" Cloe cried. "Mia said she was doing a lunch panel with him today. I bet we can catch them if we head over now."

Since they hadn't eaten lunch yet, the girls and their new director friend grabbed some sandwiches and took a table at the back while Mia and Xavier, along with a couple of other actors from *On the Edge* and the movie's writer and producers, gave a talk about making an independent film.

Cole pulled a notebook out of his messenger bag and jotted down some of Xavier's tips.

"Cole, you've already made an independent film," Jade reminded him.

"Yeah, but I can always use more ideas on how to make it work," Cole explained. "I mean, he's made a lot more movies than I have."

"It's always smart to learn as much as you can from people you admire," Sasha agreed. She pulled a small notebook out of her bag and started taking

©MGA

notes as well. When she noticed her friends raising their eyebrows at her, she just shrugged. "What? I might want to make a movie someday."

When the talk was over, they made their way through the crowded room to the front table, where Mia and Xavier were still chatting with the rest of the panel members.

"Hi, you guys!" Mia called when she spotted the girls.

"Hey, how are you feeling?" Yasmin asked.

"Oh, I'm totally fine," Mia said, waving her hand dismissively.

"Why would something be wrong with you?" Xavier asked.

"I just had a little accident on the ski slopes today," Mia replied. "It was nothing, really."

Cole muttered, "I think I'd better get

going-" and started to hurry off, but Cloe grabbed his sleeve.

"Xavier, we'd like you to meet our friend Cole," Cloe declared. "He's a director, too."

"Oh, sure, I heard your film was really good." Xavier shook Cole's hand, and Cole's face lit up. "I'm going to a screening of it tomorrow."

"Oh - thank you!" Cole stammered. "I'm really looking forward to seeing your movie, too."

"Yeah, well, I hope you get a chance to," Xavier replied. "It's not looking so good right now."

"What do you mean?" Jade asked. "Isn't a new copy on its way?"

"Look outside," Xavier said. "I don't think anything's getting in today."

The girls turned to see huge snowflakes

falling in thick sheets and settling in billowy drifts on top of the snow that already covered the ground.

"How pretty," Yasmin murmured.

"Sure, it's pretty," Xavier agreed, "but it's not exactly good news for my movie."

"It'll be okay," Cloe reassured him, but as they watched the snowdrifts grow higher and higher, they all worried that things wouldn't be okay at all.

CHAPTER 9

"It's kind of cool to be snowed in at a ski lodge, right?" Yasmin asked, looking out of the window of their room at the snow-coated world outside.

"It's beyond cool – it's freezing!" Jade joked, and her friends groaned at her pun.

"Well, since we're stuck in here anyway, maybe we should try to come up with a new suspect," Sasha suggested. "Since our first one turned out to be a real sweetheart, and there's still no sign of the missing movie or Mia's attacker."

Sasha settled into an overstuffed blue chair, and Yasmin sat in the chair next to her.

"Well, what are the possibilities?" Yasmin asked.

Cloe and Jade perched side by side on their bed, facing their friends.

"Could it be that projectionist, Derrick?" Cloe suggested.

"Nah – he loves this festival, and he loves his job," Sasha replied. "I don't think he would do anything to jeopardize that."

"I agree," Jade said. "Actually, I'm starting to wonder if Xavier might be behind all of this."

"That's crazy!" Cloe cried. "Why would he want to sabotage his own movie?"

"Just think about it," Jade insisted. "I mean, he's had way more publicity since his movie disappeared than he ever would have had if anyone had actually seen his movie."

"And the press was totally interested in Mia's accident, too," Sasha agreed.

"Well, he is tall and thin, just like Cole,"

Cloe admitted. "That could have been him on the slopes."

"And now that they can't see it, everyone's desperate to watch that movie," Yasmin added. "People were talking about it before, but now they're like, obsessed."

"All right, we'll see what we can dig up on him tomorrow," Sasha declared. "For now, why don't we order some room service and find ourselves a chick flick to watch on TV?"

"Wait, haven't you seen enough movies already this weekend?" Jade protested.

"There's always room for one more!" Sasha insisted, and her friends all giggled as they settled in for a cosy night.

When Sasha woke up the next morning, the room was bright with sunshine and the alarm clock read 10:25.

"Oh no!" she cried.

"Wha-what is it?" Cloe asked groggily.

"We totally overslept and missed our morning movie!" Sasha leapt out of bed and started rushing around, trying to decide what to wear.

"Sasha, it's okay," Jade told her. "There are plenty of other movies we can see."

"Yeah, but we're supposed to be covering everything we can for the magazine," Sasha protested.

"We've already been to a star-studded party, seen a ton of cool movies and met lots of amazing people," Yasmin reminded her. "And we still have most of the week left to go. So I think we'll have plenty of material."

"Maybe you're right," Sasha agreed. "But we still have to move it so we can make it to our eleven o'clock movie. And then we have to track down Xavier and get him to confess."

The girls got dressed quickly and dashed out of the door, making it to the cinema just before the movie was about to start. At first, they didn't see any empty seats in the packed cinema, but then they spotted Xavier waving them over.

"I was saving seats for some of my crew, but they just called and said they couldn't make it," he explained, gesturing to the four seats beside him. "And it looked like you could use some seats, so I thought you might like to join me."

"We'd love to!" Cloe exclaimed.

The girls sat down next to him and Xavier added excitedly, "You'll never believe it, but they got the movie reel here today!"

"Xavier, that's fantastic," Jade told him. "But I thought we were totally snowed in?"

"Well, some of it melted this morning, so some planes were able to land," he explained. "And one of them had my movie on it!"

"Do you know yet when it'll be showing?" Sasha asked. "We've heard so much about it – we have to check it out!"

"Isabella worked us in tonight, actually," he said. "I can't tell you how relieved I am – I thought I'd completely lost my chance to screen this movie at the festival." When the girls looked at him, they noticed that tears were welling up in his eyes. "It's just really important to me that I get this movie out there."

"That's great, Xavier," Yasmin said. "We'll be there tonight."

The lights dimmed

©MGA

and the movie began, ending their conversation. But while Xavier's eyes were on the screen, Jade leaned over to Sasha and whispered, "I don't think it's him."

"Me neither," Sasha agreed. "He seemed way too excited about getting his movie back - and way too upset when it was gone. We can keep an eye on him, but I think it's someone else."

Yasmin shushed them and the girls sat back to enjoy the show, but they couldn't stop wondering - if Xavier wasn't behind the accidents, who was?

The girls were getting dressed up for take two of the *On the Edge* premiere when Yasmin suggested, "Maybe it's Isabella."

"What are you talking about?" Jade demanded, pausing in the middle of fastening one of her gold hoop earrings into her ear.

"Think about it," Yasmin insisted as she pulled her hair back into a loose, low ponytail. "She was desperate to get press coverage for the festival, and like you said, it's had tons more coverage since the problems started."

"She does have the only other key to the projection booth," Sasha pointed out. She pulled on her tall black boots and added, "She would've had plenty of time to switch the reels."

"I don't believe it," Jade protested. She checked out the earrings in the mirror and then grabbed a belt to accent her dress. "She's a totally impressive, utterly together woman. I just can't see her doing something so completely out there."

"Besides, she couldn't have been the man on the ski slope," Cloe chimed in. She adjusted her lariat necklace so it fell just above the neckline of her dress, and then added a gold cuff bracelet to match.

"But she could've hired someone," Sasha added.

"No way," Jade replied.

"Well, let's at least keep an eye on her, okay?" Yasmin offered. "She'll be at the premiere anyway, so we might as well see what we can find out."

"I feel like we're grasping at straws," Jade complained.

CHAPTER 10

"It's a good thing we can sit in the press section," Sasha said, "because I don't see a single open seat in the rest of the cinema."

"I know - people are queuing out of the door," Jade replied. "It's standing room only in here!"

"Definitely way more crowded than the original screening," Yasmin pointed out.

"These pranks really do have everyone talking about this movie," Cloe agreed. "I just hope it's as good as they're expecting."

By the time the movie started, people were packed into the aisles and all along the back wall, and more had been turned away. The press section was overflowing - folding chairs had to be added to make room for everyone who wanted to cover Xavier's movie.

When it ended, the entire audience leapt to their feet, applauding as loudly as they could.

"That just might be my favourite movie ever!" Cloe gushed, and her friends had to agree.

"I'm so glad everything worked out for Xavier," Jade said. "He's a huge hit!"

"I'm glad it worked out for Mia, too," Yasmin added, and just then, Mia ran up to them, jumping up and down with excitement.

"Look at all these people here – can you believe it?" she shrieked. "Didn't you just love it?"

"It was amazing, Mia," Yasmin agreed. "Congratulations on all of this."

A reporter tapped Mia on the shoulder and

she whirled around, a huge smile on her face.

"Hey, there's Isabella," Jade pointed out.

"We'll catch up with you later, okay?" Sasha told Mia, but she didn't seem to notice. The girls wove through the crowd until they reached Isabella, who was just finishing an interview of her own.

"Girls, are you having the most wonderful time?" Isabella asked. "Isn't it just fantastic how this is all working out for Xavier? I know he was so worried, and believe me, I did some serious freaking out – I mean, a mistake like that, at my festival? But now it's all okay, and I couldn't be happier."

"Still no sign of those original reels, though, huh?" Sasha asked.

"No – and you girls haven't turned up anything either?" When the girls shook their heads, Isabella continued, "Well, thanks for trying. I guess it worked itself out anyway."

"But don't you want to catch the thief?" Yasmin insisted.

"Yeah, and Mia's attacker?" Cloe added.

"Well, of course." Isabella scanned the room distractedly, but didn't pause in her rapid-fire speech. "But the local police haven't found anything, and you girls haven't found anything, and I just don't know what else to do."

"Don't worry," Jade told her. "We aren't giving up."

"Thank you, really - that's great," Isabella told them. "Now, if you'll excuse me, I need to make sure my staff are all set for tomorrow."

With that, she flitted away, her long, orchid-patterned dress fluttering behind her as she hurried through the throng of movie goers.

The girls looked at each other and Jade sighed. "I'm not convinced. But you guys are right - this has been good for the festival. So we can't rule her out, either."

"Well, the awards are tomorrow," Sasha reminded them, "so that would be the perfect time for the prankster to strike."

"The awards are tomorrow?" Cloe gasped. "You mean, the festival's almost over already?"

"I know, I can hardly believe how fast it's gone," Yasmin agreed. "But we're sticking around for the screenings of all the award winners the day after the ceremony, so we have a little more time left."

"But we've hardly had time to do anything yet!" Cloe wailed. "I mean, we haven't even had time to go snowboarding!"

©MGA

"We'll try to fit it in before we go," Sasha told her. "But in the meantime, we have to solve this case!"

"I bet I know where we can track down some really good clues," Jade said.

"Where?" her friends chorused.

"At the big Actors' Association party tonight!" she declared. "We're already dressed to impress, so we might as well get out there and strut our stuff!"

"Yeah!" her friends cheered.

The party was fabulous, but by the time they got home that night, they still weren't any closer to solving the mystery.

"I bet you're right, Sasha," Yasmin declared. "I bet whoever it is will mess something else up at the awards ceremony. And when they do, we'll be there to catch them in the act."

Everyone at the entire festival was crammed into a single, huge auditorium the next evening to find out who this year's big Starshine award winners would be.

"Xavier has to win," Jade whispered.

"I really hope Mia gets a prize too," Yasmin added.

"Ooh, and Cole," Cloe chimed in.

Isabella strode onto the stage to announce the first award, which was for the audience favourite.

"And the winner is ..." She opened the envelope in her hand and exclaimed, "*This is My Life*, a film by Cole Larkin!"

As the crowd cheered, Jade murmured, "Good for Cole."

"Xavier and Mia will be totally bummed, though," Yasmin pointed out.

But just as the winning director began to

make his way towards the stage, all the lights went out, plunging the whole auditorium into utter darkness.

A wave of worried murmurs swept through the auditorium, and then the dim emergency lights that lined the aisles flickered on, illuminating poor Cole, who stood frozen halfway to the stage, and Isabella, looking completely stunned onstage.

"Well, I guess it can't be Isabella," Yasmin admitted.

"I'm glad," Jade said, "except that now we're back to square one."

"Everyone, due to the electrical outage, we'll have to resume the awards ceremony at nine o'clock tomorrow morning," Isabella shouted.

Her microphone had gone out with the rest of the electricity, so she had to yell to be heard throughout the auditorium. Everyone groaned, but began filing slowly towards the exits.

"Don't worry," Isabella continued, "we'll still have time to show all the winning movies afterwards."

"I think that's the least of her worries right now," Sasha muttered, and her friends had to agree.

CHAPTER 11

The girls were almost back to their hotel when Mia caught up with them.

"Can you believe that?" she asked. "I mean, what is going on at this festival?"

"I wish we knew," Yasmin said sadly.

"Hey, you girls aren't going to bed, are you?" Mia continued. "Tonight's the official Starshine party - everyone will be there!"

"We probably should cover it for Bratz Magazine," Jade pointed out, and her friends nodded tiredly.

"Do you want to meet up in the lobby and head over together?" Cloe asked their new friend.

"Totally!" she agreed. "Just call my room

when you're ready, and I'll hop on down."

Back in their room, the four best friends examined their wardrobes, each trying to come up with one last glamorous outfit.

"How about this?" Cloe suggested, holding up a sparkly black gown.

"Gorgeous!" her friends declared.

"Okay, if you're glamming it up, then why don't I wear this?" Jade grabbed a silver dress and did a little twirl with it.

"Perfect!" her friends proclaimed.

"Ooh, you girls are a tough act to follow," Yasmin complained. "But I have a little glitz up my sleeve, too." She grabbed a gold strapless dress and added, "Ta-da!"

"Love it!" her friends cheered.

"All right then, I guess I'll have to go with this one," Sasha announced, producing a shimmering white gown from the wardrobe with a flourish.

"Fabulous!" her friends exclaimed.

"Well, that was easy," Jade said.

Although it had taken only a few minutes to choose their outfits, the girls spent the next hour primping - picking out accessories, doing their make-up and styling their hair. They were so into their beauty rituals that they didn't realize how much time had passed until Cloe glanced at the clock and gasped.

"Oh no! Mia's gonna think we totally ditched her," she cried.

"Come on, Cloe," Jade reassured her. "Mia's an actress - she knows how long it can take to look utterly fabulous."

But just then the phone rang and Cloe lunged for it.

"Hello? Oh, hey, Mia, we were just - oh,

really? Of course! We'll be right there."

She hung up the phone and turned to her friends, a grim expression on her face. "Girls, we have a fashion emergency on our hands."

All four girls took one last glance in the mirror before heading for the door and down the hall to Mia's room. Sasha knocked lightly, and when Mia opened the door, they were shocked to see that she was still in the sweater and jeans she'd been wearing earlier that day.

"Omigosh, you all look incredible!" Mia exclaimed. "And I'm a total disaster."

"Mia, what happened?" Yasmin asked as they entered the room and took in the piles of clothes that covered every surface.

"I couldn't decide what to wear," she said sadly. "I tried everything, but nothing seemed right. And you girls always seem so together that, well, I was hoping you could help."

"We sure can!" Jade declared. "Fashion is our speciality!"

"Now, let's see what we've got here." Sasha began sorting through the piles of clothing, setting aside all the jeans, skirts, sweaters and T-shirts, and pulling out every dress she could find. Mia sat in the middle of her bed, watching hopelessly as her friends took control.

Cloe headed for the bathroom, where Mia had

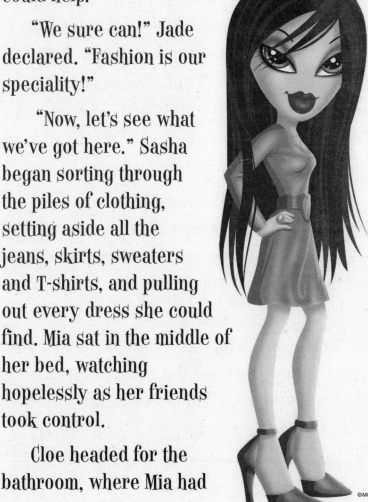

©MGA

thrown make-up and hair products all over the countertop. Cloe started opening compacts, picking out only the richest, most glamorous shades for a lush evening look.

Yasmin checked out the top of the dresser, where Mia had spread out gorgeous, glittering necklaces, earrings, bracelets and rings. "Well, at least we aren't dealing with an accessory shortage."

Jade went into the wardrobe, which in Mia's sprawling suite was a luxurious walk-in. There she found a jumble of shoes and almost nothing else – Mia had tossed the rest all over her room.

"I can work with this," Jade declared, and began digging through the shoes, searching for strappy, sparkly high heels.

"What about this dress?" Sasha called, and the girls converged to examine a glittery burgundy dress.

"Ooh, that's amazing," Mia gushed. "How did I miss that before?"

"Well, you did have a lot of other stuff in the way," Sasha pointed out.

"Go and try it on," Yasmin suggested. "And try these ruby earrings and necklace with it - I think they'll match perfectly."

"I have just the right make-up look for you," Cloe added.

"And I'm sure I can find you some shoes that will look great," Jade said, heading back to the pile in the wardrobe.

She had spotted one burgundy shoe and was digging around for another when she saw something that really didn't belong in a wardrobe - a big, metal circle that looked an awful lot like a movie reel.

"Yasmin, can you help me for a minute?" she shouted.

Yasmin hurried over.

"Is that what I think it is?" Jade hissed, gesturing to the reel in the shadows at the far corner of the wardrobe.

Yasmin clapped her hands over her mouth, shocked.

"I think it just might be," she murmured.

"Did you find me some spectacular shoes?" Mia asked, emerging from the bathroom in her little dress.

"Still working on it," Jade told her. "But I did find something else I thought everyone might like to see."

With that, she yanked the reel out of its hiding place and stalked back into the bedroom, holding the reel up for everyone to see. Her friends gasped, while Mia seemed to shrink into herself in the middle of the bed.

"How - how did that get there?" she

whispered.

"You're a good actress, Mia," Yasmin said, appearing behind Jade. "But you can't act your way out of the cold, hard truth."

CHAPTER 12

"How could you do it, Mia?" Cloe cried, her blue eyes wide with shock. "How could you sabotage your very own movie?"

Mia burst into tears, and although she was angry, Yasmin handed her a tissue.

"I just – I just wanted to be noticed," Mia sobbed. "I was so tired of just being a teen star. I wanted people to see me as a real actress! And I figured if I could make it big at Starshine, everyone finally would."

"I always thought you were a real actress," Yasmin said quietly. "In fact, you were my favourite movie star. But now, I'm not so sure."

"I wasn't trying to ruin the festival," Mia insisted. "But I thought if the movie could get more buzz, then everyone would be talking about me, too. And it worked! Except then talk was dying down, so I got a friend to stage my 'accident' so I could be the centre of attention again. And that worked too! But when Cole won instead of Xavier - well, I didn't know what to do. I thought if I could take the focus off of his film and get people talking about everything that kept happening to Xavier's movie again, maybe it wouldn't matter that Cole had won. Because the prizes are important, but it's the buzz that sells movie tickets."

"Cole will still get the award tomorrow, though," Jade pointed out.

"I know, I know," Mia wailed. "But I had to do something!"

"No, you didn't," Sasha told her. "You know you're going to have to turn yourself in-"

But Yasmin cut her off.

"What you've done isn't okay," Yasmin told Mia, "but it also isn't the worst thing in the world." Sasha started to protest, but Yasmin held up a hand to stop her. "I mean, think about it. No one got hurt, Xavier can have his reel back, and his movie - and the festival - got more publicity than ever. So despite your bad motives and worse techniques, things may have actually worked out for the best."

"Does that mean that you aren't going to turn me in?" Mia asked with a sniffle.

"I mean, what would be the point?" Yasmin turned to her friends, her brown eyes pleading for their understanding. "She did give an awesome performance in that movie. And yes, it would have got her plenty of attention without all this scheming. But she got scared and made a mistake, and if we tell on her, it will ruin her career. Do you really want to be responsible for that?"

The girls exchanged looks, and finally Jade said, "It's up to you, Mia. If this is really a secret you want to keep, it isn't our place to spill it."

But Mia shook her head. "No. I've caused enough trouble already. It's time for me to come clean."

All five girls walked over to the party together, their glitzy gowns hidden under warm wool coats. Mia carried the film reel under one arm, and none of the girls said anything as they approached the hall where the party was being held.

"Well, here goes," Mia said as she pushed open the doors. As they dropped off their coats at the front, Mia spotted Xavier across the room. "Wish me luck."

"Good luck," the girls replied. They watched as she strode over to Xavier and waited nearby, eager to hear how she would explain herself.

"I have something of yours," she began, holding the reel out to Xavier.

"Oh, wow!" he exclaimed. "Where'd you find it?"

"I didn't find it, exactly," she admitted. "Actually – I'm the one who took it."

"You what?" Xavier cried. "Why would you do something like that?"

"Honestly?" she said. "I was just trying to help."

"By ruining our premiere?" he demanded.

"By getting everyone talking about our movie!" she told him.

"But they were talking about it anyway," he reminded her. "I can't believe all this time

114

you had it right here. And I was so upset, thinking someone was out to get me – and it was you, all along."

He stalked off, but she followed him, grasping the sleeve of his suit jacket. "Xavier, I'm so sorry. Please, let me explain."

While the girls watched, Mia told the director how desperate she'd been for the movie to be a hit, and how it had all just spiralled out of control.

"Well, I'm glad that you cared that much about the movie," he admitted, "but really, pranks and thievery are not the best way to promote a film!"

"I know, I know," she murmured. "I made a huge mistake, and I understand if you

©MGA

never want to work with me again. I don't think I'd want to work with me again, either."

"You messed up pretty bad," Xavier told her, "but you also did the right thing by telling me. You didn't have to do that. And as for working with you again, well – I actually already have a role in mind for you in my next film. If you promise never, ever to do anything like this again, the part's still yours."

"I swear!" Mia exclaimed, and then motioned her friends over to share the good news. "These girls helped me realize that honesty is the best policy," she explained.

"Thanks, girls, for everything," Xavier told them. "I'd love for you all to be my guests at the VIP wrap party tomorrow – all the biggest names will be there, and I'll be happy to introduce you to anyone you want to meet."

"That would be amazing!" Cloe squealed.

"For the next issue of our magazine we

could use a few more celebrity interviews," Jade admitted.

"Then it's settled," Xavier declared. Just then, he saw Cole step into the room, looking lost, and waved him over. "Congrats on your win tonight!"

"I'm sure you'll win plenty more tomorrow," Cole replied modestly. "Your film completely blew me away."

While the directors talked about their craft, the five girls headed for the dance floor, where they twirled and spun beneath a glittering disco ball, giggling and chatting until late into the night.

As they all headed home that night, Yasmin slung an arm around Mia and said, "You did a good thing tonight," and Mia smiled, relieved that her mistake hadn't cost her her newfound friends.

The audience could hardly sit still at the awards ceremony the next morning. Most of them didn't know that the mystery of the festival prankster had been solved, so they were all waiting for the next thing to go wrong. But this time, when Isabella took the stage and announced Cole's award, he made it to her side to finally claim his prize.

"I can't thank y'all enough for choosing my movie for this honour," he declared. "I'd be thrilled if the judges liked my movie, but it means even more to me for my audience to love it, because you're the ones I made it for!"

Everyone applauded wildly, and the girls grinned at each other.

"What a sweetie!" Cloe exclaimed.

Next, Isabella announced the judges' pick for best picture – it was *On the Edge*, Xavier's film! He dashed down the aisle and practically leapt onto the stage, wrapping Isabella in a huge hug when he reached her side.

"I love Starshine, I love my cast, I love my crew, and I love all of you!" he shouted, and the audience laughed and cheered as he ran back to his seat, holding his trophy high in the air.

"He totally deserved it," Jade whispered, and her friends nodded.

The girls didn't know the rest of the award winners, but they perked up again when they heard that the next prize was for best actress.

"And the award goes to ... Mia Mackenzie!" Isabella announced.

Mia hurried onto the stage and took the microphone, while her friends cheered her on.

"I wouldn't be here without the help of my incredible director, Xavier Redman, and also my wonderful friends, Cloe, Jade, Sasha and Yasmin," she said. "Girls, come up here – this award is for you too."

The four best friends turned to each other, surprised. It wasn't like Mia to share the spotlight! But they were totally honoured, so they made their way to the stage and took a quick bow at their new friend's side.

They met up with Mia after the ceremony and she said, "You girls were totally right. If I'd just believed in myself instead of trying to force people to pay attention, everything would have worked out fine anyway."

"We all have trouble trusting our talents sometimes," Yasmin replied. "I just hope that from now on, you'll trust yours, because you're truly amazing!"

Mia gave her a hug, and soon Cloe, Jade and Sasha joined in for one big group hug.

"You four have done so much for me this past week," Mia told them. "Isn't there anything I can do for you?"

"Two things," Cloe replied. "First, come snowboarding with us in the morning."

"Done!" Mia cried.

"And second, give us an exclusive interview for the next issue of Bratz Magazine," Cloe added. "We'll put you on the cover if you'll give us the inside scoop on the life of a movie star."

"Absolutely!" Mia exclaimed. "I'll tell you anything you want know - even the true story of how I almost destroyed my very first trip to the Starshine Film Festival."

So the girls got their cover story, plus tons more interviews at Xavier's party the next night. They had plenty of movie reviews and party coverage, as well as features on snowboarding and skiing.

And when they got home, their report cards were waiting for them. Despite their hurried studying, they had all got straight As!

And when they got home, their report cards were waiting for them. Despite their hurried studying, they had all got straight As!

"Let's meet at the office to write up these stories while they're still fresh in our minds," Jade suggested. "And then I think we deserve a trip to the mall to celebrate our fabulous film festival adventures."

"Not to mention our amazing grades!" Sasha added.

"And of course our best magazine issue ever!" Cloe declared, and although Cloe tended to get carried away, her friends all had to agree that this time, she was absolutely right. The Starshine Film Festival Special Issue was, without a doubt, going to be the most spectacular issue of Bratz Magazine yet!

Read more about the Bratz in
these other awesome books!

Pixie Power
Spring Break Safari
Diamond Road Trip

BRATZ
Magazine

the magazine for girls with a PASSION for fashion!

ALL THE LATEST BRATZ & CELEBRITY NEWS!

ALL THE BEST FASHION TIPS & ADVICE!

COOL FEATURES, COMPETITIONS, POSTERS & MORE!

U.K. Customers get 1 issue free!
13 issues for only £29.25
Order online www.titanmagazines.co.uk/bratz
or call 0870 428 8206 (Quoting ref BRZPA1)

U.S. Customers Save 35%!
6 issues for only $19.50
Order online www.titanmagazines.com/bratz
or call 1 877 363 1310 (Quoting ref BRZPA2)